# ALEX
## has had
# ENOUGH!

## Nicole Johnson Mockler
### Illustrations by Sean Mockler

Published by:
**FriesenPress**
Suite 300 – 852 Fort Street
Victoria, BC, Canada V8W 1H8

www.friesenpress.com

Distributed to the trade by The Ingram Book Company

**Dedicated to all the kids who**

**are or have been bullied**

## TO ALL PARENTS/EDUCATORS

This book has been written to help young kids realize the seriousness of bullying. It has also been written to help parents and teachers address the issue with children. This book could be used as part of the class curriculum for grades 3, 4, & 5. Once the students have all read the book, the teacher could make it an opened discussion with the students.

## ENDORSEMENTS

"All schools would benefit from having this book in their library to help them with their anti-bullying initiatives. Parents can use the book to help them discuss the subject with their children. Bullying needs to be prevented before it starts. Our children's healthy development depends on it."
— *Angela Mancini, Chairman of the English Montreal School Board*

"Bullying is a serious problem which starts early and continues on to all aspects of life. Addressing, helping and empowering children at a young age are ways to do prevention. This book is a good tool for parents and educators."
— *Louise da Silva, Teacher at the  secondary level*

"This wonderful book not only deals with bullying but with multiple children's issues: trust, friendship, single parenthood, body image and feeling 'different'. So many children will identify with Alex and Alice! In a very sensitive way, the author allows the young readers to explore strategies for themselves."
— *Louise Bergeron, retired school principal*

"This book sensitizes children and parents to the realities of a child who is being bullied. It provides clear guidelines for empowering a victim."
— *Bonnie Goodman Conrad, MSW, NYU, school social worker*

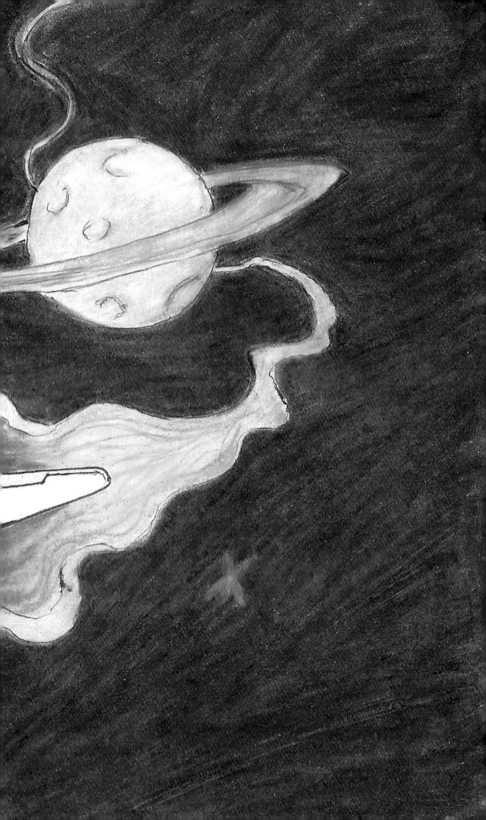

# - ONE -

## ALEX HAS HAD ENOUGH

After spending three months on Mars, Alex is in his space ship returning to Planet Earth. He is the Astronaut who was selected by NASA to visit and report on Planet Mars.

He is always excited to return to Earth and tell about his adventures and about the nice inhabitants of Mars. At the same time, he is also sad about returning to Earth where he believes people can be very mean. In his space ship, he feels on top of the world. He laughs to himself, "I am on top of the world".

He navigates through the dancing clouds, looking across the universe that is unbelievable and breathtaking. The sun is shining on his face. He is anxious as he approaches Cape Canaveral and gets ready to land. He wishes that he could remain in the sky forever and continue to feel as light as a feather. But, as a famous astronaut, he knows that the reporters are waiting for him impatiently. When the door of his space ship opens, camera lights flash, coming from all directions, instantly blinding him. Reporters call out questions to him.

"Alex, tell us all about your adventures on Mars."

"Alex, what are the people on Mars like?"

"When is your next voyage?"

Click! Click!

"Smile. Alex!"

# - TWO -

"Alex. Alex. Wake up, it's time to get up and get ready for school."

Alex is confused. He wonders who this is. He opens his eyes and realizes that it is his grandmother.

"Get up, big boy! I have prepared your favorite breakfast, French toast with maple syrup."

Alex gets up. He does not care what clothes he wears. He puts on pants that are too small and his favorite sweater that doesn't smell very good.

"Who cares? I like it," he says to himself as he sits at the breakfast table ready to devour his French toast.

There is so much maple syrup that he can hardly see the French toast.

His grandmother hugs him and says,

"Hurry Alex, you are going to miss your bus again and your mother is going to be upset."

Alex doesn't really feel like going to school but he knows he has no choice.

# - THREE -

On his way to the bus stop, Alex thinks about his new life since his move to Montreal. He remembers being happy in Toronto. He liked his French immersion school, had many friends, and was even on his school's soccer team. However, at the beginning of last summer, his mother had announced that they were moving to Montreal to live with grandma.

Since he has been living with his grandmother, he has gained a lot of weight. She loves cooking for him. He likes living with his grandmother but more than ever; he misses his Dad. Alex's Dad died when Alex was only two years old.

It has been hard for Alex to make new friends here in Montreal. He is the only kid of his age on his street and somehow it has been very difficult to connect with kids at his new school, except for Alice.

Unlike the other kids, Alice is the one who accepted him from the very beginning and they are now good friends. Alice is Korean so she knows what it is like to be different and knows how Alex feels. Alice told Alex that she had a hard time with certain kids when she first started school. She talked to her parents about it and they helped her to deal with it. When someone would tease her, she would change the subject by telling him or her about her talents in karate.

Alex does not want to worry his mother and has not been able to come up with any talents he could show to Tony and his friends. Alex is too afraid of them.

# - FOUR -

Alex arrives at his bus stop and is happy to see Alice. He is often very worried about coming face to face with Tony.

"How is it going, Alex?" says Alice.

"Fine, I guess," replies Alex.

They climb into the bus as Alex makes a big effort not to look at anyone. He and Alice sit behind the bus driver and the first voice Alex hears is Tony calling,

"Hey, it's that big fat Alex." Tony's friends laugh.

"Just ignore him," says Alice, but this is very difficult for Alex. He knows that

Alice still gets comments that upset her, especially, when they refer to her as being Chinese.

She firmly replies,

"I am not from China. I am from Korea and I know karate. Would you like to learn some techniques?" This seems to work for her. Numerous times, she has made Alex laugh so much when she demonstrated her karate movements. Alex wishes he were as courageous as Alice, when she confronts bullies.

# - FIVE -

Alex is in class and his teacher, Madame Suzie, is teaching English. Alex has difficulties staying awake, as he doesn't always sleep well at night. When he does sleep, he loses a lot of his energy traveling to planet Mars. Alex puts his head down on his hand and falls asleep. He is soon on Mars meeting with Chief Otti, a very gentle man who is always happy to see Alex.

"How come the people of Mars are always so nice?" asks Alex. Chief Otti contemplates the question and answers.

"The most important law of our planet is to respect one another," replies Chief Otti.

Alex is about to respond when he hears,

"Alex! Alex! Where are you?"

It is Madame Suzie's voice. He is all confused and quickly responds,

"On Mars!"

Now the whole class is laughing. He would like to simply disappear. He knows very well that Tony and his gang will torment him even more.

Later, when Alex goes to the washroom, he realizes that Tony and his friends are waiting for him. Tony gives him a push and says to his two other friends,

"Hey, this is the guy from planet Mars. Are there tough fat guys like you over there?" Alex quickly leaves wondering why those guys always find Tony so funny.

# - SIX -

Alex is feeling very sad and thinks about Alice's advice to go tell an adult. He wants to talk to his teacher but decides to go to his locker and get his lunch box. His grandmother has put four cookies in it. He eats two of them asking himself, "When will all this end?"

In the bus on their way home, Alice notices that Alex is very sad. Once they get off the bus, Alex decides to tell her all about the washroom incident. She is upset.

"Alex, enough is enough! You need to tell an adult. I can go to the principal with you, if you want."

Alex doesn't reply and Alice tries to make him laugh. "All right, let me show you some new karate techniques that I learnt yesterday. Here is what you are going to do and this time, try to listen and learn." She proceeds to do karate kicks, left and right. Alex is really determined to learn but after a couple of kicks, he falls flat on his rear end. Alice, who has a good sense of humor, also drops onto the ground and both start to laugh. Alex knows that when Alice laughs too much, she ends up having the hiccups. The more they laugh, the more she has the hiccups.

# - SEVEN -

Once at home, Alex's grandmother is waiting for him with a huge snack. He knows very well that one of the reasons why Tony and his gang bully him is because of his weight. However, he cannot resist the cookies and the chocolate milk. He feels very sad. His mother works long hours and his grandmother watches a lot of television.

He gets on his old bicycle and leaves the house without really knowing where he is going. He pedals and pedals, remembering that while in his school bus, he has seen a path that leads to a small wooded area. He begins to feel tired and reminds himself, "Too many of grand-ma's cookies." When he lived in Toronto, he did a lot of physical activities, soccer and street hockey with his friends. He has nothing like that anymore. He finally reaches the wooded area, knowing very well that it is not safe for him to be there alone. He puts his bicycle down and sits, leaning against a tree, and almost immediately falls asleep.

Again, he is in his space ship on his way to planet Mars. This time Chief Otti is waiting for him.

"I was quite anxious to see you again, Alex. How are you doing?"

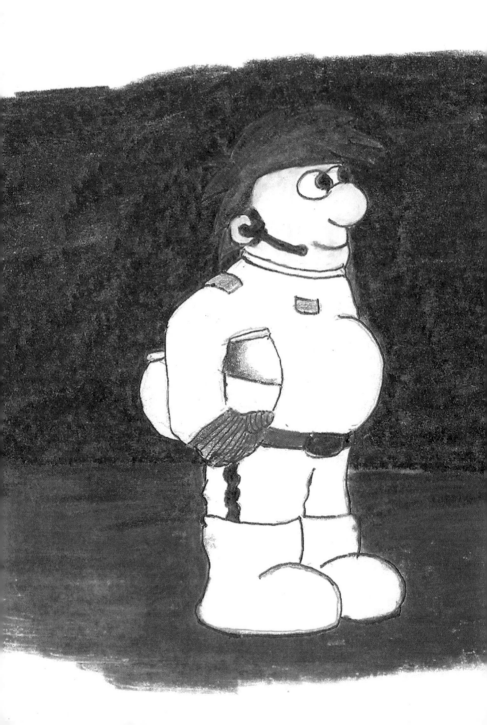

This time Alex decides to tell the Chief everything about his difficult life on planet Earth, his sadness since he has moved to Montreal, the fact that he is continually victimized by three guys, his weight problem and so on. Chief Otti listens attentively and responds,

"You know Alex, there is good and bad in each of us. What is important is to find the good in every one and to help them discover it for themselves." Alex is thinking.

"But how do I find it when I constantly live in fear?"

Chief Otti would like to give Alex the answer but he knows the importance for Alex of discovering it by himself. However, he does give him a hint.

"Your friend Alice, she has succeeded, yes?"

# - EIGHT -

Alex suddenly wakes up.

"That's right! Alice followed her parents' advice and showed her strengths by using her voice and body. She has demonstrated her talents and has demanded respect. That is what the Martians expect from one another, respect.

Alex, wide-awake, realizes that it is getting dark. He has no idea of the time but he knows that both his mother and grandmother must be very worried. He climbs onto his bike and suddenly hears a funny sound.

He says to himself,

"That didn't sound like it was coming from the forest." He stands up and

realizes that his pants just ripped at the most embarrassing spot. He laughs to himself.

"If Tony ever saw this, boy would he have a field day with me!"

When Alex gets home, he is surprised to see a police car, his mother and grand-mother, the neighbors, even Alice and her parents, all outside waiting. When they see him, everybody runs to him. His mother and grandmother are cry-ing and hugging him so tightly that he

has a hard time breathing. He is also trying very hard not to show his torn pants.
Constables David and Lewis approach
him and explain to him that Alice has
told them everything about his harass-
ment at school.

They are very nice, as well as are the
neighbors who were concerned for him.
He remembers Chief Otti's voice saying
to him,

"There are good people everywhere."

Alex's mother and the detectives discuss the situation. They agree that tomorrow morning, they all will go to Alex's school to address the bullying issue with the principal.

Alex is not concerned anymore because he has made the decision that he has had enough and he will demand respect. Alice comes to see him to give him a hug. Alex impulsively decides to tell her about his torn pants and he even turns around to show her.

Alice, who tends to be very giddy by

nature, starts to laugh and laugh, and then, of course, the hiccups start. Alex joins in and all are looking at them when Alex turns around and shows his backside. Everybody is laughing, even the police officers.

Alex's mother points a finger at her mother, laughing. She says,

"No more junk food and sweets for this guy except on special occasions. Alex needs to go back to playing sports and get more exercise. He is going to show them all what he can do."

# - NINE -

For the last two weeks, Alex had been preparing for a class presentation. Of course, his subject is, "Is planet Mars inhabited?" That night, before going to bed, he reviews all his presentation, the beautiful pictures he found by himself on the internet and his own drawings. He has no doubts; it will be a good presentation because he knows all about Mars. After all, he goes there often, even if it is only in his dreams.

The next day, as planned, Alex, his mother and one of the detectives meet with the principal and his assistant at the school. Alex listens attentively and discovers that all police officers work very hard at addressing the problem of bullying in schools. Alex asks them to give him the chance to act on his own. He no longer wants to be a victim. After explaining to them, all agree with a plan to support him. Alex intends to start by showing his talents.

# - TEN -

Once in class, it is time for the presentations. Alex asks Madame Suzie, the teacher, to let him give his presentation first. Alice wants to be second.

Alex does his presentation on Mars. He describes the voyage that takes you to the planet, the universe, the dancing skies, and the brilliant stars. As he talks about everything, he shows spectacular images and his own drawings of Mars and its inhabitants. He tells the class about Chief Otti, about their ways and values, and all about their kindness and respect for one another. During his presentation, all eyes and ears are on him, except for Tony and his friends. Then Alex notices that even the friends are listening, despite Tony's attempts to distract them. The presentation is over. The whole class applauds Alex. Would you believe even Tony applauded?

"Superb job Alex," says the teacher.

"Bravo!" says someone else.

"It really sounds like he's been to Mars," replies another.

Alex smiles to himself.

# - ELEVEN -

It is Alice's turn. She is wearing her costume from Korea. She salutes in the Korean way and tells about her history of adoption. Then she presents beautiful pictures of her country of origin, along with a Korean dance. All of a sudden, she removes her costume, and underneath it is her karate costume. She explains all about karate and its self-discipline of the body. Then she proceeds to charmingly demonstrate the karate movements, leaving the class in awe. All applaud her and as she goes by Alex's desk, they give each other their secret sign of friendship.

The other students proceed to do their presentations. Then it is Tony's turn. He is very nervous but manages to maintain his tough guy attitude. He is not well prepared on his subject of hockey and mumbles the words. The teacher reprimands him.

"Tony, you don't seem to be prepared for this presentation."

The other students laugh but Alex remembers Chief Otti's message about finding good in everyone. Alex puts his hand up to ask a question.

"Tony, I have seen you many times playing hockey. What position on the ice do you usually play?" Tony is surprised and he quickly responds to Alex's question trying his best to explain the various positions in hockey. A few girls are getting annoyed.

"We are not interested, this is a dull subject."

"Everyone has the right to present and be treated with respect," replies Madame Suzie. "Tony has chosen to speak about

hockey. Everybody should listen. Please proceed, Tony."

To everyone's surprise, Tony admits to not having prepared for this presentation. Since his parents' divorce, he says he finds it hard to live in two different homes.

Alex puts up his hand again and makes another suggestion.

"How about if we asked Tony some questions about hockey?"

Madam Suzie agrees and the questions begin. Tony is suddenly up to par answering them all with knowledge. Once the presentations are finished, Madame Suzie congratulates her class about their support for all their classmates. The principal has informed Madame Suzie about this morning's meeting with Alex's family and the police officer to address the fact that Alex has been a victim of bullying by other students. She takes the opportunity to explain the importance of respect for each other. She talks about how the lack of respect can come in different forms. She tells them about ways of showing respect for one another. The whole class is very attentive.

At recess, Tony and his friends come to see Alex and Alice. Tony is the first to apologize to Alex. They have a friendly exchange of handshakes between the boys and Tony proposes a hockey game after school.

Alice is upset,

"And what about me?"

The others look at her and Alex says,

"With everything she knows about karate, I think it would be a good idea to ask her to join us." The boys laugh and agree. Alice is happy and replies.

"Well, in that case it will be in front of my house at four o'clock. Bring your equipment; I will supply the lemonade."

# - TWELVE -

At suppertime that night, Alex's mother and grandmother talk to him about how sad they were to find out that he had gone through so much in silence. They wished they had paid extra attention to him. This allows Alex to tell them about his feelings, how sad and lonely he has been since his move to Montreal. He even tells them about his dream of visiting Mars and about becoming an astronaut one day. He also announces his wish to play hockey in the winter and soccer in the rest of the seasons. His mother is very happy.

"I have kept all the information on soccer registration but it is up to you to get the information on hockey." His grandmother adds that she will pay for his hockey equipment.

"You know Alex; your grandfather was quite a hockey player in his time. Let me dig up his old hockey pictures and we will look at them after dinner. Alex gets excited about this.

"I bet he was a good player like me."

"He sure was," replies his grandmother.

That night, Alex is in bed thinking about all that has happened since the

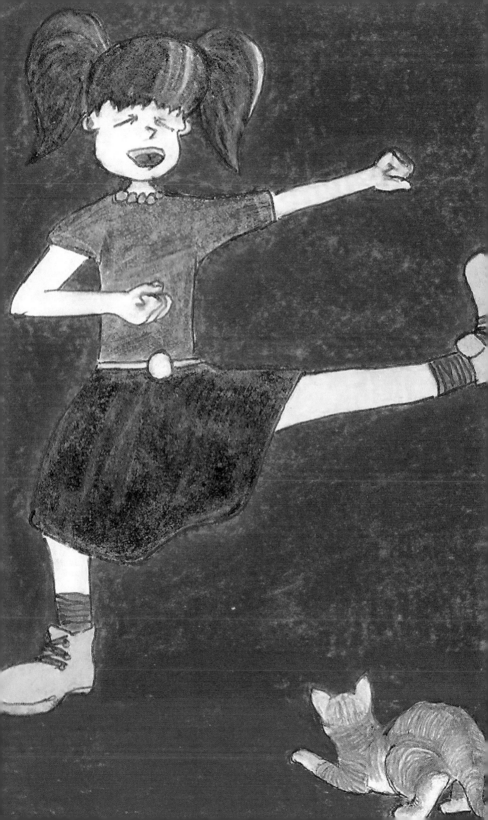

morning and since he has moved to Montreal. He makes the decision that never again will he allow anyone to disrespect him. Chief Otti's advice has served him well and he thinks that maybe he will no longer feel the need to escape to planet Mars. One thing for sure though, he will one day be an astronaut and maybe he will travel to the unknown. You never know, maybe he will really go to Mars. For the time being, what he knows for sure is that when you have had enough, you have had enough! He showed his strengths and proved that he deserves respect.

That night Alex dreamt about his friend Alice showing him her new karate technique. A grey cat was watching them. He wondered if it was Chief Otti. It felt very comforting. When he woke up in the morning, for the first time since his move to Montreal, he was looking forward to going to school.

# - END -

# IMPORTANT MESSAGE TO ALL KIDS WHO ARE BULLIED

Bullying can take different forms like name calling, making fun of how you look, pushing, hitting you and any other ways that make you feel badly. **REMEMBER, NOBODY HAS THE RIGHT TO HURT YOU SO TELLING AN ADULT IS VERY IMPORTANT.** Here is what you can do to make it stop:

1) The first time someone tries to bully you, you inform that person about what your skills are.

Example: "I am pretty good at playing ball. Do you want to play catch?"

2) If this person bullies you again, you look at that person and firmly say, loudly and clearly,

"I want you to stop."

3) If this person continues, you say it

again.

"I want you to stop right now or I will go tell someone." <u>It could be the principal, the teacher, or any adult</u> you trust. It is very important that you tell an adult.

These three first steps are called "empowerment". A big word that means you are taking charge.

4) When you tell someone, it is important that you also tell that adult about all the things that you have tried to do to stop the bullying.

5) If that adult does not do anything about it, you continue to tell another adult until he or she has truly listened to you and done something about it.

**REMEMBER, TELLING YOUR PARENTS IS ALSO ONE OF THE BEST THINGS TO DO**

## IMPORTANT MESSAGE TO THE ONE WHO BULLIES

Bullying is wrong! It must stop! You may not be feeling good about yourself. Maybe you are going through hard times and harassing someone makes you feel big and tough. Bullying is bad for you and your victim. It is very important that you go talk to someone about it. Ask an adult you trust to help you find that someone.

# QUESTIONS FOR THE STUDENTS

1. What did you think of Alex?
2. Which words do you believe define Alex the best: sensitive, scared, imaginative, determined, talented, courageous?
3. Do you think Alex would have been bullied if he had not moved to a new city?
4. What words would you use to describe Alice?
5. Why do you think Alice managed to stop the bullying?
6. What is your opinion about the guidelines suggested to stop someone from being bullied?
7. Do you know someone who is being bullied?
8. How do you think you can help to stop the bullying?

# FROM THE SAME AUTHOR

A series about "LINA" is in preparation. Lina is a rambunctious four years old girl who lives with her Mother, Father, her brother and their dog Maxi. During the day, while Lina's parents are at work, Lina goes to daycare and her brother Justin is in grade two at his neighborhood school.

The collection about "Lina" tells stories to children, while teaching them the importance of safety, kindness, and respect of others.

The stories also help parents learn and adapt parenting strategies useful in various situations.

## LOOK FOR THE FOLLOWING IN BOTH ENGLISH AND FRENCH

- LINA DOES NOT WANT TO GO TO SCHOOL
- IT'S DINNER TIME FOR LINA AND HER FAMILY
- LINA DOES NOT WANT TO GO TO BED
- LINA GOES IN 'TIME OUT' TO REFLECT
- LINA SAYS: "MY BODY BELONGS TO ME!"
- LINA KNOWS ABOUT GOOD AND BAD SECRETS

## STAY TUNED FOR MORE!

CPSIA information can be obtained
at www.ICGtesting.com
228949LV00003B